MW00912380

WEALTH OF DECEPTION

Written by: PAULINE TOMESKI

Created by: JOHN PAUL McLAUGHLIN

WESTBOW®
PRESS
A DIVISION OF THOMAS NELSON
& ZONDERVAN

Copyright © 2014 Pauline Tomeski.

All rights reserved. No part of this book may be used or reproduced by
any means, graphic, electronic, or mechanical, including photocopying,
recording, taping or by any information storage retrieval system
without the written permission of the publisher except in the case
of brief quotations embodied in critical articles and reviews.

Cover image by David Tomeski

WestBow Press books may be ordered through
booksellers or by contacting:

WestBow Press
A Division of Thomas Nelson & Zondervan
1663 Liberty Drive
Bloomington, IN 47403
www.westbowpress.com
1 (866) 928-1240

Because of the dynamic nature of the Internet, any web addresses or
links contained in this book may have changed since publication and
may no longer be valid. The views expressed in this work are solely those
of the author and do not necessarily reflect the views of the publisher,
and the publisher hereby disclaims any responsibility for them.

Scripture taken from the New King James Version.
Copyright © 1979, 1980, 1982 by Thomas Nelson,
Inc. Used by permission. All rights reserved.

Any people depicted in stock imagery provided by Thinkstock are models,
and such images are being used for illustrative purposes only.
Certain stock imagery © Thinkstock.

ISBN: 978-1-4908-6278-1 (sc)
ISBN: 978-1-4908-6279-8 (e)

Library of Congress Control Number: 2014921856

Printed in the United States of America.

WestBow Press rev. date: 12/19/2014

This book is dedicated to:

Our great and awesome

Father

The Son

and

The Holy Spirit

1 Timothy 6:9-10 But those who desire to be rich fall into temptation and a snare, and into many foolish and harmful lusts which drown men in destruction and perdition. For the love of money is a root of all kinds of evil, for which some have strayed from the faith in their greediness, and pierce themselves through with many sorrows.

Acknowledgments

To my wonderful husband David, my brilliant daughter Claudia and my forever inspirational son, John Paul

Chapter 1

Looking out the window into complete darkness, Jeff, is in deep thought on how his life could be so different if he had money. His daughter, Rachel, needs braces and he is thinking how great it would be if only he could write out a check and pay the orthodontist. Life would be great without thinking about the bottom line of his check book, he could pay the car insurance, water bill, electric bill and pay off those high credit card bills without thinking twice. Soon the property taxes are due, where will I get the money for that? There is never enough, never. The more Jeff thought about what he didn't have the angrier he got.

Retirement? Get serious, that is gone!! Jeff thinks to himself, I had to pull out my 401K to cover unexpected expenses. The last storm we had ripped off part of the roof with the 100 mile an hour winds and the water damage was more than anyone expected. The house insurance did not cover all of it. Anytime I put money in savings something comes up. I don't even have $500.00 in the bank. His thoughts were fueled with anger until he exploded with the words "Why God is there never enough? Don't I deserve more? Am I not a wonderful person?"

Jeff sits down and places his head in his arms and tries to figure this thing out.

Depression was setting in. It has been years since he has been on a family vacation. We use to have so much fun on vacation. Julie and I would watch the children play in the ocean's warm water and build castles in the sand. We would rent a beach house on the ocean and watch the sun go down every night. We would bond as a family and always talk about how we wanted to come back the next year. The years rolled by and we never made it back to the ocean. I love the ocean. I have thought of going back so many times just never had the money.

Jeff gets into bed and lays next to his wife, Julie, of 25 years but can not sleep.

After several hours of tossing and turning, Jeff still can not fall asleep. He gets up and goes onto the porch. The rain has stopped. It is a clear night and he could see the stars shining brightly. Jeff stares into the heavens and sees the full moon. It is so beautiful, so magnificent that it takes his breathe away. He thinks on how, "In the beginning God created the heavens and the earth." God had made the two great lights that is written in Genesis 1:16, "The greater light to rule the day and the lesser light to rule the night." God also created those awesome stars that twinkle so brightly. Jeff cries out to the Lord, "God help me, my only desire is to have more enough money to exist without struggling. I am sick of not having enough."

Grief overwhelms Jeff. His eyes fill with tears, feeling hopeless. He will be turning 44 years old in a few months and the burden of "not enough" sickens him.

Jeff thinks, "If only I had money, I would be a much better person. I would be able to do so much more than I do now. I would be able to feed the hungry and provide wells for clean water in places where the water is not fit for drinking.

I would be able to help my church. I would be able to help my Mom, she has been struggling since my Dad has died. I could help people all over the world, if only I had more money."

Jeff is tired and goes back into bed. Julie reaches out to him and tells him to be happy with what he has. A family that loves him.

"I love you, honey" she whispers in his ear. "Love is better than riches." Julie kisses Jeff and they fall asleep.

Jeff was born on the south side of Chicago where he lived with his father, Jerome, and his Mom, June until he married Julie. His father died from a heart attack right after Jeff and Julie had their first born son. They decided to name Jerome after Jeff's Dad.

His father was a locksmith and worked for a small company on Archer Ave not far from their house. Jerome walked home from work many times. All the neighbors knew him. Jerome was very friendly and on his walking trips home many people would stop and talk to him. Jerome was the best locksmith Chicago had ever known. He could fix any lock and could open any door in less than 60 seconds.

Jerome would be called in to help the police open safes or locks when no one else could open them. Jerome loved to work together with the Chicago Police Department.

Jeff's Mom stayed home and took care of the children and the house as they were growing up. June loved to garden and cook. Many times Jeff would come home from school and smell fresh bread baking or have cookies warm from the oven. Jeff's Mom would can her vegetables she grew in her garden. There was always an abundance of vegetables so Mom would give them away freely to their neighbors. Jeff's parents were loved by many.

Jeff stands tall at 6 feet. He is rather handsome with black curly hair. He is a good man. Loves his wife, Julie, and his three children. Jerome is his first born son, Jake is his middle child, and Rachel, the youngest is the joy of his life. Jeff seems happy on the outside but inside he is in turmoil. His yearns for the peace, the peace that surpasses all understanding, but does not have it.

Jeff is a manager at a small computer store. Jeff hates his job. His boss, Carl, claims to be an atheist and is always testing Jeff's faith and knowledge of Jesus Christ. They have long discussions about religion and instead of Jeff's faith strengthening he finds it weakening. Sometimes he would come home from work and really think that Carl was right. Where is God when you need him?

Julie was also born and raised in Chicago. Julie's Dad's name was Jake and her Mom's name was Joyce. Both Julie's Mom and Dad worked for the city of Chicago. Jake was the Zoning Commissioner and Joyce was a Real Estate Agent, specializing in the downtown neighborhood of Chicago. They died together in a suspicious car accident not that long ago.

Julie is 5'5 with flowing short blond hair. She is a God fearing woman. She is the anchor in the family. She always wants to do what is right, reads her Bible every day and is a wonderful wife and mother. She is an encourager. She has a part time job at their church as the church planner for upcoming events and guest speakers. Julie is 3 years younger than Jeff. They are childhood sweet hearts. They met at a church carnival that was held in late summer. At first glance they both fell in loved. They always blamed it on the glitter of the lights that festive night in October. Jeff was 18 and Julie just turned 15 years old. Since they have met their eyes were only for each other. They were married a few years later and moved to a small town south of Chicago.

Jeff and Julie spend a lot of their time together. They enjoy each others company. They make a good team. They also have shared many heart breaks but their love for each other held them together and made them strong.

Julie will never forget when Mom and Dad came over the last time before she learned of their death. The day was wonderfully warm for the fall. Julie thought it would be a great day for a Bar-B-Que. The children were there and everyone was happy to be together. Is was not often everyone got together including Jeff's Mom. It was the best time for everyone.

After dinner Julie's parents decided to tell them about the changes that were going to take place in one of the poorest parts of Chicago. Her parents were working together on a deal that was for a large amount of land just outside of the downtown area. Julie's mom was working for the real estate company that wanted to purchase the land that was going to be used for a sky scrapper and a large parking lot. It was zoned for residential and there were people living in very old houses. A few were boarded up with vagrants living in them. They were in the process of finding out who owned the property. Her father was working together with the Administrator changing the zoning from residential to commercial. There were a lot of problems. Most of the families who lived there could not afford to move. The people started to picket and shouted "Don't take our land!" Julie's father did not want to take the property from these poor people. They have no money and no where to move to. They could find another place to build the skyscraper. Julie's Dad refused to change the zoning from residential to commercial. There was nothing the zoning commissioner could do.

After Julie's patents left their home they received a call from the police that her parents were in the hospital. As Julie got to the hospital both of Julie's parents were dead. They died in a mysterious car accident. There were no witness on what exactly what happened. Jeff was not home.

The officers wanted to know more about this real estate deal that Julie's Mom and Dad were in but Julie only knew what her Mom told her – they had not discussed any details. The police suspected the mysterious car accident had something to do with the rezoning of the property. To this day they never found the connection of the death of her parents with the real estate

Chapter 2

After another restless night Jeff gets up in the morning to the smell of bacon and eggs. His wonderful wife, Julie is up early getting things ready for her family to start the day. She smiles as Jeff comes down the stairs.

"Good morning my dear" she states as she hands him a cup of coffee. Jeff kisses her gently on her forehead. "Feeling better?"

The day is sunny and already hot and Jeff is feeling much better. On his way to work he stops at the local convenience store and picks up the paper and decides to buy a lottery ticket. It would be so nice if I would win and get rich, Jeff thinks to himself.

Jeff forgets about the ticket and after a few days he finds it in his pocket. He checks the numbers and he is the winner, the only winner of $500,000,000. Jeff can not believe it!! He looks and looks and looks again. He is afraid to tell anyone even his wife. A day goes by and then he finally tells his family. They sit around the table planning on how to spend their new fortune. The first thing Jeff says is that he will quit his job and encourages Julie to do the same. We can travel and buy a new bigger house. Jerome and Jake could go to the college of their choice. Rachel can have beautiful clothes and her own play room for all her toys. Everyone could have their own TV's in their room.

Julie thinks of opening up a small business in town. It would be a fabric shop and she would also carry yarn and arts and crafty things. Woman would gather once a week and take lessons on how to make something or learn to knit. It would be a gathering place where they would also pray for one another. Maybe hold afternoon Bible studies. She mentions it to Jeff and he is neither for it or against it. All Jeff could think about is what he plans on doing with his money.

Jerome mentioned that he wanted to be a lawyer and help people who did not have a lot of money. Jerome's heart is towards helping people. He is a kind and generous person.

Jake wants to learn how to fly. He would travel all over the world and stay at islands and drink tropical drinks all day. His interests are with the here and now.

With money, almost all things were possible. Jeff was not sure on how much money to give each son, so things went somewhat back to normal until the decision was made.

At first the money was a blessing. He pays off his house, credit cards and buys two new cars. One for himself, and one for Julie. Of course Rachel gets her braces, not just any braces but the top of the line braces. The best of the best. Jeff bought a new yacht for family vacations and a plane to travel all over the world. Jeff decides to move his family into a mansion on the hill where all the rich people live.

Jeff rides in his new car, through his new beautiful neighborhood. He marvels at the trees; they are so big and mature. He could not imagine what these houses look like inside so big, so beautiful, each different from the other. The houses are not close to one another, each sits on a minimum of two acres and the landscaping was absolutely beautiful!. He never dreamed that he and his family would live here.

"Look at me!!!!" he shouts. "I am driving a new Mercedes, living in a fine house! Look at me! I have no debt, money in the bank and have money in my pocket!! Everyone wants to be me!"

Jeff's thoughts of power rule his mind. He is into politics now and knew the mayor and other high officials. Many people with much influence were his friends now. He would want or lack for nothing! Jeff thinks of himself as the greatest!

Chapter 3

Jeff and his wife take a trip to see Jeff's sister Jamie. She lives outside of Chicago in a north suburb. His sister is newly divorced and lives in a small house with a big mortgage. Jeff only has one sister and loves her dearly. He hands her the check a $1 million dollars so she can have anything she wanted. His sister is over joyed and is speechless. They hug with tears of joy in their eyes. She could not stop thinking on how she was going to spend her new wealth. A bigger house or should I pay off this one? Go back to school or open up a new business? So many decision and what fun decisions that have to be made. Jamie could not stop thanking them for their generosity.

After lunch with Jamie, Jeff and Julie got into the car and start heading back home. They were so excited about the happiness they saw in Jamie's face. This will give her a great new start to get her life back in order again after the divorce. Jamie will be able to meet new friends and go to new places. Her life will have a new meaning. Jeff looks at Julie and smiles. "I am so happy that we could make a difference in Jamie's life", said Julie.

The next day Julie and Jeff decide to take a trip to their first born son, Jerome, who is in his second year of college and give him a check for $1 million dollars. Jerome is a straight A student. He enjoys living away from home. As they handed Jerome the check he instantly decides to quit school. Jeff tries to talk to him about finishing school and be that lawyer he always wanted to be. "I want to enjoy the money", states Jerome. They hugged and said good bye. It was Jerome's life and now his money and they drove home. Julie says to Jeff," I hope we did not make a mistake by giving him that much money." "Me too," agrees Jeff.

As fast as he cashes the check Jerome starts to gamble, thinking he can easily double his money. Jerome thinks that he could take his million and make another million! His greed for money has already started.

Jerome meets a new set of friends at the casino with his new found wealth. They party and get high all the time. Jerome buys a boat so they could drink and do their drugs without being bothered. When he is not on the boat he has his new Corvette. Jerome drives around town picking up pretty women. He now has plenty of time and money. Fast cars and fast women become the norm. Jerome is very generous to his new set of party friends. He pays for their drinks and buys his new girlfriends beautiful expensive jewelry.

Julie calls Jerome and tries to talk to him about investing his money and going back to school. Jerome refuses to listen to his Mother. Julie reflects on how Jerome use to be. Jerome was so smart and had a wonderful way with people. He had the gift of generosity. It made Jerome happy to be able to help people. Now he was using this money to buy his friends drugs and alcohol. What a waste of money and life. Jerome thinks that the money would never stop coming in and that he would keep on winning money when he gambled. Jerome was on top of the world with his winning streak and new friends.

Jeff and Julie hope when they gave Jake his million dollars things would go better. Julie and Jeff go and see Jake in college. As they hand him the check Jake decides to transfer into a much better college. For this they are much grateful. The three of them sit and talk for awhile. As they decide to leave, Julie asks her son to please be wise in his decision making.

Jake gets into a new college and he joins a fraternity. Jake starts to party and never stops. He uses his money to pay other people do his homework. Jake gets introduced to a variety of drugs his life is in a spiral downfall. He is drinking alcohol from the time he gets up to the time he passes out. He gets arrested with DUI charges. Jake uses his money and influence to buy his way out of it.

Jake buys a small used plane and learns to fly. He is spending his money faster than he expected. His friend hears about a great stock to invest his money in. Jake takes the advice of his friend and invests in this cheap stock. Later he loses that money too!

Jake is not much of a leader, he enjoys being with people who take the lead. He is easily influenced. He is just about out of money after just a few months.

Rachel is only 8 years old. Jeff is not sure what to do for his princess, so Jeff puts her million in a trust fund until she is 18 years old.

Jeff and Julie take Rachel shopping and she gets a new bedroom set for her huge bedroom. The room next to her bedroom is her new toy room filled with old and new toys. She sets up her table and chairs and asks her Dad and Mom to have tea with her. They both come to the tea party, eat cookies and enjoying each others company. Rachel is so happy to be with her Mom and Dad and wishes this moment will never end. Little did they know this would be the last time the three of them spent time together.

Chapter 4

Rachel has her Mom's blond hair and blue eyes. She has the smile of an angel and when she smiles the world lights up. Rachel came late in the marriage and was a very pleasant surprise. Julie was told she could no longer have children. She had a miscarriage after the birth of Jake and never would be able to get pregnant again. After a few years went by she got pregnant with Rachel. Overjoyed were Jeff and Julie as they heard the good news. Rachel is very petite and is treated like her Daddy's princess.

Rachel and her Mother live together in this huge house on the hill. Jeff seldom comes home. Rachel and Julie go to church together and join together in many activities. They pray for Dad and her two brothers every night before bed. Rachel no longer feels like her Daddy's princess. From time to time Jerome and Jake call and check up with them about how things are going. Rachel loves her brothers and wishes she would see them more often.

Today is Rachel's 9th birthday. She has a small birthday party at school. Mom made Rachel's favorite rainbow cupcakes to take to school and share with her classmates. Julie is planning a very special dinner with her brothers. Dad is also invited but no one expects him to come.

School calls Julie and asks Julie to pick up Rachel she is not feeling well with a high fever. Julie drops everything and goes and gets Rachel from school. Rachel is burning up with a fever. Julie takes Rachel right to the emergency room at the local hospital. They rush Rachel right in. She is vomiting and her fever has jumped to 105 degrees. The doctors and nurses are working on Rachel to get her fever down. They are trying to find out what is wrong with her. It must be some kind of super bug.

Outside Rachel's room her mother is calling up everyone she knows to pray for Rachel. Several Church people arrive and they are joined in prayer for Rachel's healing. Jerome and Jake are in the waiting room, sitting in silence. Fear grabs Julie, Please Lord, don't let my daughter die!

Julie goes back into the room where Rachel is. She looks down on her only daughter and listens to her labored breathing. The doctors can not find out what is wrong with Rachel. Julie is holding Rachel's hand and whispers to her, "Don't be afraid, our heavenly Father is with us."

Suddenly Rachel sits up and says to her Mom, "Mama do you see the Angel?" Julie looks around and does not see anything but a brilliant shining light. The light was so bright that Julie is blinded by it.

"What does the Angel look like?" asks Julie. "She is so beautiful her wings are sparkly pastels of light colors. The wings are so big that they are touching the floor. She is dress in white and she is smiling at me and says I will be fine." Jesus Christ has heard the prayers of His people. Then the Angel disappears and so does the light Julie saw.

Rachel said," I sure am hungry, Mommy." Julie calls to everyone in the waiting room to come in and see her daughter, "She is healed!! She has been healed and is ready to eat! God has healed my daughter!!!" Everyone starts to sing and dance giving God all the praise! Jake picks up Rachel and twirls her around in circles, he holds her close to him! Jerome states "Little princess, you gave us quit a scare!"

The doctor and the nurse hear all the commotion and hurry down the hall. The doctor asks, "What are all these people doing in Rachel's room?" Julie said, "An angel was here and told Rachel that she would be healed and she was! Look at her!!! She is well. God heard our prayers!!"

"Amen!!" the people shouted.

The doctor looked at Rachel. He examined her and she no longer had a fever. Her color was back in her face, Rachel was in fact better, much better. Rachel was released from the hospital with strict orders to rest for a few days. The doctor and the nurse didn't know what to make of the healing. They never saw anything like it.

When they got home they put Rachel to bed and said they would have her birthday party tomorrow. Rachel asked her Mom to call

Daddy so she could tell him about the Angel. "Sure," Julie said and she kissed Rachel good night and tucked her in. Julie looked down at her daughter thanking God for His mercy. Slowly Rachel's eyes closed and fell into a deep restful sleep.

Julie calls Jeff and it goes right to voice mail. She leaves a message knowing that he will not return her phone call. He must have forgotten about Rachel's birthday. How could he?

Jeff is on his docked yacht wrapped up in the arms of his new honey. The warm breeze gently comes into the portal. Outside it is another perfect day here in the Islands. Jeff hears his phone ring on the dresser. He gets up and looks at his cell phone. He sees it is from Julie. His first thought was how could she bother me, she knows I don't want her calling me. She probably wants money.

Jeff takes the cell phone into the galley and gets another cup of coffee. Anger fills him and he turns the phone off and throws it down on the counter thinking, "I will deal with her later!" He puts his coffee down and switches to something stronger.

Jeff downs his drink and suddenly from the corner of his eye he sees a shadow. As he starts to turn around two masked men come on board and with guns drawn they ask Jeff to turn over his money or they will shoot him. Jeff is surprised and can not think. One man puts the gun to his head and asks him for his wallet and his jewelry. Jeff immediately gives the man holding the gun his watch and his wallet. While one man collects the items from Jeff the other man goes down below the deck and collects whatever else he could find. Jeff's girlfriend is hiding under the bed. She is shaking and forgot her cell phone so she can not call the police.

The masked man looks around and heads up the stairs. When he reaches the top of the stairs both men leave the yacht. They jump into a get-away car and take off. Jeff makes sure his girlfriend is OK and calls the police.

Jeff is so upset he can not think. The police ask him to describe the two robbers and asks them to come to the police department to look at some mug shots. Jeff had to make a report on what was taken. In all the chaos Jeff forgets to call Julie back. Jeff and his girlfriend filled out all the paper work at the police station and decided to go shopping. After all Jeff can not be without a watch. In fact he bought a better watch then the one that was stolen and a diamond belt buckle to match. Of course Jeff's girlfriend wanted a bigger and better set of ear rings and a new diamond ring. They both were back on the yacht and admiring their new jewelry before the end of the day.

Jeff said to his girlfriend it is so nice having money. It makes life so much easier and off they sailed into the sunset on a two million dollar yacht! Jeff said "Life is good!" and his girlfriend just nodded her head in agreement.

Chapter 5

The next morning when Rachel got out of bed, Jerome and Jake were already downstairs waiting for her with a birthday surprise. Rachel jumps into the arms of her brothers and kisses them both.

"What do you have for me?" Rachel says with expectancy in her voice and a big smile on her face.

Jerome says, "You have to guess. What is brown, black and white and will sleep in your bed?"

Rachel repeats "Sleeps in my bed????"

"Hummmmmm need another clue?" Jake asks. "She will play with you for endless hours, and will lick your face!"

Rachel smiles and says, "Is it my very own dog???????????"

"You got it!!!" everyone shouts in unison.

Julie took her by the hand into the living room and led her to a huge box wrapped up in shiny gold paper. She opened it up and there was the cutest beagle puppy she ever saw. The puppy licked Rachel face and cuddled up to her. "I love you," Rachel said and kisses the puppy. Her name will be Angel after the Angel I saw in the hospital.

Rachel still has to rest for a few days, she feels great and now has little Angel to keep her company.

While she is resting in her new pink canopy bed. Rachel remembers on how things were before the money. Things were so nice. The family had dinner together every evening and on the weekends they played games. They use to have "Family Day." After Church they all would go to the forest preserve and spend the day fishing and having a picnic lunch. The house was small so everyone was always near. Now Daddy is never home. The house they live in now is so big now it takes her awhile to find her Mom. Her heart feels heavy. Her eyes fill with tears. Rachel feels very lonely and misses her brothers too. Angel comes up to her and licks the tears from Rachel's face. Rachel pets her beloved friend and thanks God for all that she has experienced in the last few days, her Angel, her healing, and her new dog.

Rachel gets out of bed and goes down the winding stair case. Angel follows her. Rachel sees her piano in the front room and decides to play. Playing the piano has always brought her peace. She recalls the day she got her piano; it was a gift.

Rachel always wanted to learn to play the piano. Rachel asked her music teacher if he would teach her to play on the school piano. He agreed. Knowing they had no money, he would teach her for free. Rachel's family could not afford to buy her a piano. The church saw how well Rachel played the church piano. She truly had a gift from God to play so beautifully. The church decided to have a bake sale as a fund raiser to purchase a piano for Rachel. They had signs along the highway to advertise their goods. A couple saw that sign and came in to buy a pie. When they heard it was a fundraiser for this little girl they asked to speak to the girl's mother. When Julie approached the elderly couple they told her that they had a piano in storage and they could have it free! Rachel has been praying for a piano and here these great people gave them theirs.

The church was so happy to hear about Rachel's piano and this generous couple. The Church decided to use the money from the bake sale for repairs for the church which were so badly needed.

When it is time for Rachel to go to bed, Mom comes in to read Rachel a story. Mom knows right away something is wrong,

"What's the matter honey?"

Rachel looks at her Mom tearfully and says, "I miss Daddy. He would always tuck me in and kiss me."

Mom answers and says "He will be home late."

Mom reads Rachel the Bible story of David and Goliath. As she tucks Rachel in, she tells her she must be strong like David fighting Goliath and trust in God. God will make things good again, she reassures Rachel.

Mom gives Rachel a hug and kisses her good night. She sits with her for awhile in the dark also thinking about the way things used to be.

Chapter 6

Jeff decided to come home. It has been almost two weeks since he has been home. He smells of alcohol. It is very late. Julie pretends she is sleeping. Jeff undresses and passes out next to her and is snoring in seconds flat. Julie lays there wondering how long she could take this new Jeff. Praying about what she will say to him tomorrow morning. They must talk.

Morning comes and Jeff joins Julie at the kitchen table. Rachel has left for school already. Julie pours Jeff some coffee and ask him what he would like for breakfast. "Nothing," he states.

Julie pauses and softly asks, "Where have you been for the last few weeks? I have so much to tell you." She takes a seat at the table and looks at Jeff.

"Honey, Rachel, misses you. She cried herself to sleep last night. She misses you reading to her and tucking her in. She is doing very well in school. Tonight is Parent Teacher conferences and she would like you to be there. She worked very hard and won a few awards and is very proud of her accomplishments."

Jeff gives a slight shake of his head and replies, "I have things to do tonight and I can not be there."

"What is so important that you can not be there?" Julie questioned.

Jeff"'s eyes turn black and he looks away from Julie and states, "I am important now and have things to do and places to go. The mayor has invited me to his house for drinks and maybe a game of golf." Jeff heads for the door.

Julie stands up and reminds Jeff that Rachel has a piano recital next Sunday. "Please be there, you will break her heart if you're not."

Jeff does not say anything and reaches for the door knob when Julie says, "Before you leave, we have to talk. Please sit down." Jeff looks at Julie with disgust. "What is it that you want? Make it fast! I can not keep the mayor waiting!"

Julie sits down and takes a sip of her coffee. "We have a lot of money now and I suggest we should give some of the money to people in need, maybe we could start a ministry?"

"Ministry!" Jeff shouts. "I don't have time for ministry. Everybody wants something from me."

Julie continues, "We always talked about helping the poor, now we can actually do it!"

"No!!" shouts Jeff. "Do what you want, but leave me out of it!"

"Well what about the church?" Julie asks. "They are in need of money because of the damage done by the storm awhile back."

"They never did anything for me why should I give them anything?"

"Jeff," Julie pleads, "we cannot be just takers. We have to give." Jeff just shakes his head no.

Julie can see the difference in Jeff. He is becoming arrogant and argumentative. Jeff always made time for family things before they had money. Now that he has a lot of money he no longer has any interest in family or the things family do. His greed for money has made him selfish and self-centered.

Julie notices the new expensive watch and the diamond belt buckle to match. Julie tries to reason with Jeff and states, "Your spending is out of control and the money is not going for anything good." The more she tries to reason with Jeff he gets more and more upset with her. Jeff gets into her face and says through gritted teeth, "It is none of your business what I spend my money on." That is when Julie smells woman's perfume on her husband.

Julie questions him about the smell of perfume. In a fit of anger Jeff starts to scream at Julie. Julie accuses him of cheating on her. He pushes Julie against the wall and storms out the door yelling out loud, "I have money now, I could have any one and any thing I want! Leave me alone!!!!"

Chapter 7

A week goes by. Julie and Rachel have not heard from her Dad. Rachel misses her Daddy very much. She calls him several times and he does not answer her calls or returns her messages. "Please come home, Daddy. I want you to come to my piano concert," Rachel pleads.

Rachel has been practicing for hours to show her Daddy how well she can play. She leaves another message. Jeff does not reply.

Jerome calls his Mom and Rachel to find out the details of the event. He assures, "Jake and I will be there. In fact we wouldn't miss it for the world."

"Please call your Dad, Jerome, and remind him about the concert. Rachel really wants him to be there. It would be nice that all of us as a family would be together. How about going out for Pizza afterward to celebrate?!"

"Sure thing, Mom, I will call him right away."

Jerome calls his Dad and when Jeff see's it is his son he picks up the phone.

"Hi Dad, I am so happy that I got a hold of you."

Jeff asks Jerome, "Is there a problem?"

"No, Dad nothing, I just wanted to remind you that Rachel has a piano concert and all of us would like you to be there."

Jeff is silent on the other end of the phone. After a few seconds, Jeff states, "I would love too but I have a very important meeting and I will not be able to make it." There was disappointment in Jerome's voice and he states "Dad we all miss you and want you to be part of our lives, but you are never here."

"I am sorry son," says Jeff, "it is what it is. I will not be there." Jerome felt great pain in his heart as they said their goodbyes and hung up. Jerome wondered if he would ever see his Dad again.

The night of the concert has finally come. Rachel is very nervous and looks between the curtain to see who came to see her play. As she peeks she is so happy to see her Mom, Jerome, Jake, her Auntie Jamie and her new boyfriend in the very first row. There is an empty seat next to Mom where Dad would have been seated. Rachel is devastated that her Daddy was not there. As her eyes filled with tears. Suddenly she saw something that erased the tears away and eased her pain. It was Mr. and Mrs. Jamerson!!!!! The elderly couple who gave her the beautiful piano and right next to them was Mr. Collins, her music teacher! It was because of them that this is all possible!! They smiled at Rachel and waved. What a wonderful sight to see. This couple made it possible for Rachel to have a piano of her very own and free lessons from the music teacher at school. They have given me this beautiful gift I will in return give them back my gift of my piano playing. Their gift was not wasted. She loved her piano and does not want a new one.

Rachel came out on the stage. The stadium went silent. Rachel started to play. The music flowed with such power that all of heaven opened up. It sounded like a heavenly angel was playing. The music filled the concert hall. As Rachel played the music pieces of Bach and Beethoven there was not a dry eye in the place. As she came to an end of the concert she stood up and took a bow. The crowd went wild with applause. "Encore!!" they shouted. "Encore!" The applause of hundreds of people thundered though out the stadium. "Encore," they shouted again! Rachel smiled to the audience and sat down and played "Ode To Joy," giving God all the glory for giving her this talent.

The news reporters were there and took her picture. An article about Rachel having this beautiful gift at the age of 9 years old was on the front page of the paper the next day. What a great night to remember. They all went out to eat Pizza afterward including the Jamersons to celebrate Rachel's concert. The absence of her Dad was not mentioned.

Jeff is on his yacht in the Caribbean partying with his new set of friends. Wine, women and song. He is dancing to a new set of rules. He lives only for the moment. Jeff forgets about the

Lord, his wife and his children. Jeff does not have a care in the world.

After a few days after the concert, Julie has been trying to call Jeff for hours. Where could he be? "Lord God in Heaven," Julie cries out to the Lord, please have Jeff answer his phone! Julie frantically is trying to reach Jeff again. Julie just found out Jeff's only sister, Jamie has died.

Finally, Jeff answers his phone. Julie softly tells Jeff that his sister was found dead in her home on the north side of Chicago from an overdose of heroin. The needles were laying next to her body. Her boyfriend was also found dead next to Jamie.

Jeff returns home. He reads the police report regarding his sister's death but decided to investigate Jamie's death himself. The neighbors say that Jamie kept to herself most of the time. Jamie and Jack were living together and grew more and more recluse after just a few months of being together. What prompted one of the neighbors to call the police was that Jamie's dog was outside over night and the next day. The dog did not stop barking. The dog was usually inside with them and seldom barked.

The neighbor knew something was wrong and called 911. There the police found the two dead bodies next to each other. As the police enter the house it was apparent they were using heroin for some time.

Jeff is at the morgue first trying to sort things out. Jeff looks at his sister's body. Jamie was so thin and frail even being dead for awhile the circles around her eyes were prevalent.

Why heroin??? What happened? My sister never used drugs. Who is this guy Jack? As it turns out Jamie had met Jack and he introduced Jamie to heroin. Having all that money Jeff had given her lead to her addiction. Reality started to settle in. Jeff gets very angry and starts to punch the door behind him. "Why!?", he screams out. "Why my sister who could have had anything she wanted!!!!" He starts to cry over the body of his sister and he blames himself for her addiction.

After a few hours he thinks how stupid she was for not using the money for something good. His attitude changes and he blames her now for being so stupid! Jeff's heart is hardening. He blames other people, nothing is ever his fault.

Julie and Rachel meet Jeff at the morgue. Rachel runs up to her Dad and hugs him not wanting to let him go.

"Daddy please come home. I miss you so much." Jeff holds her and tells her it is too late. He is going to file for a divorce from her mother. He has met a new woman. He has a new life now!

Tears flood Rachel's eyes. "What about me, Daddy?!!! I am your little Princess, I need you!" Jeff yells "It is too late! You will always be my princess." He tried to console her but his words are empty. He is not the father or the man he used to be. He loves his new live and does not want his old life to be part of him any longer. He tells Rachel to let go of him and go to her mother.

Julie sees Rachel crying and running to her. She yells to Jeff, "How could you do this to her? Have you no heart left? Every night she prays for you to come home and cries herself to sleep. How could you be so mean????" With a look of total disgust he says, "It's over" and walks away.

As Jeff steps outside he looks up and there is the most beautiful moon. He recalls the beautiful moon he saw which seems like decades ago. It was only a couple of months ago when he was talking to God about not having enough money. Now he looks up to the heavens and thinks. "I have it all now!" Jeff does not want to think of the way things used to be, just about what they are going to be.

The next few days are filled with the funeral arrangements for Jamie and her boyfriend. Jamie's boyfriend has no family. Jamie did not have any money left. It all went for heroin. Jeff decided he will pay for everything in cash. Jamie and her boyfriend did not have many friends left. Most of the people that attended were friends of Jeff and Julie. It was really a sad affair. It was over in one day and they lay to rest next to each other besides the graves of Julie's Mom and Dad.

Chapter 8

Jeff and Julie meet with the lawyers. Julie wants half of the money. He fights with her to only have child support for Rachel. He states that this is not her money, it is his. Jeff's new life now consists of only him and what he wants. Julie does not deserve any part of his money. Greed has hardened Jeff's heart and everyone sees it but Jeff. Jeff thinks he is right and the world is wrong.

Julie will not agree with only child support. They argue and Jeff storms out of the room. Jeff thinks to himself, "I will make sure she gets nothing, nothing, nothing at all."

Why does Jeff not want me to have half of the money? He did nothing to get it but buy a ticket. Why has he started to hate her? He has gone so far from God and family. Julie starts to cry and is ashamed of how her heart has hardened towards her once true love. Julie cries to the Lord, "Show Jeff what he has turned into, show him his hard heart."

As Julie leaves the lawyers office, Julie is force to admit to herself that it is over between her and Jeff. There is no turning back. She most move forward. It is over! She must reach for the future without Jeff, something she thought would never happen. Her whole life has been around Jeff and the children. Now she has to start to think about herself. What does she want to do? Rachel is still so young to be without a father. What am I to do and where to begin?

Julie gets into her car and starts to cry and the tears will not stop. It is the death of a relationship and she is mourning over her loss. We were so happy when we were broke and now we have so much money and our lives are so miserable. Julie sits in silence and calls out to God, "Lord help me, what am I to do?"

Julie decides to open up her fabric shop before Jeff takes control of all the money. This is something Julie wanted to do since she learned how to sew many years ago. After searching for weeks she finds the right place on the main street in town. She calls her new fabric store "Sewing Seeds." I will teach people to sew clothes and create crafts that will be mailed to poor people in other countries. With each article of clothing a Bible will also be sent with them. Everything will be handmade and prayed over before being shipped out. Our merchandise and Bibles will be mailed all over the world and it will be for the glory of God. We will sow seeds where no other organization can go. The gospel will be preached and The Word given out to the end of days! Julie wants everyone in the world to have a free Bible so they can be saved and come to know Jesus Christ as their Lord and Savior!

Julie plans on "Sewing Seeds" also having Bible Studies once a week. Everyone is invited. Many people will come, it is the only business in town that is offering Bible studies. "Sewing Seeds" will also be a learning place. Julie also invited other teachers over to teach people how to knit and crochet. It will be a place of happiness and joy. Christian music will be playing all the time!

Rachel is so happy because Julie asked her to be a part of "Sewing Seeds." Rachel's job will be to help pack the items up for shipping out. Rachel brings her beagle Angel to help out almost every day. Everyone is happy to see Angel. They bring her treats and bones because of what the beagle represents, that there are Angels in heaven and Rachel seen one.

Jerome and Jake helped their Mom move into her new shop and are delighted that their Mom is doing something for herself. The will have a Grand Opening where the whole town will be invited. Julie has employed five people to help her make her dream come true. All Glory to God!

After the move was complete Jerome, Jake, Mom and Rachel ordered pizza. They were tired but truly happy about this new adventure. Julie feels this will pull the town closer together and closer to God.

Finally Julie says the money will be used for good not evil. Everyone rejoices!

Jeff buys another awesome mansion overlooking the ocean where he docks his yacht. Jeff and his new girlfriend move in together. She is young and beautiful. Jeff loves the way he looks so good walking next to her. Jeff feels young again! The new honey is only interested in what Jeff can do for her like the new clothes and all the wonderful places he takes her. Jeff decorates her with beautiful jewelry from diamond toe rings to diamond jewels for her hair. Her necklace alone is worth 1 million dollars. Jeff is too busy to even think of anything else besides himself and his new girlfriend.

As time goes by Jeff and Julie are going to meet with lawyers again to talk about the divorce. Julie still wants half of his money. Jeff starts to hate Julie. "Who does she think she is?" Jeff thinks. This is my money and she gets nothing! Anything Julie says to him only fuels his anger.

The lawyers try to get Jeff and Julie to agree on something, but they do not. Jeff's eyes blacken and he storms out of the office. "Over my dead body will you get anything!" he shouts.

"Stop, Jeff," Julie cries. "Don't make this the last words you say to me! OK, I will settle for ¼ of the money." Jeff looks at Julie and says. "This money is not yours and you are not getting one penny, EVER!!!! so don't even think about it."

"Why are you so bitter to me and the children?" states Julie. "We have done nothing to you!"

Jeff answers back, "You always took everything from me. I did not even have lunch money. You took it all, now I am taking it all."

Julie looks up at him and says, "There was no money to give you! You did not make much money at the computer store. I only had a part time job! If you remember we lived on love. Love for God and love for each other and love for the children. And we trusted in God for all our needs. Somehow we always had enough."

Jeff shouts, "We never had enough. I was sick of not enough, now you want to continue and take it from me. No way Julie, you will know what it feels like to not have enough!"

Jeff looks into Julie's eyes and yells, "I hate you!!!!" and bolts out of the room, knocking over a chair and the papers that were on the table. Papers fly all over in his swift escape. Jeff is hoping he will never see any of them again!

Julie looks at the lawyers and puts her head down in her arms on the table and starts to cry. Both lawyers look at each other and don't know what to say. Julie's lawyer gets up, approaches her and hugs her, saying, "I hope we can work something out soon."

Jeff is thinking on his way to the yacht. I want Julie out of my life. He starts to consider that with Julie out of the way, he can have all the money plus the $100,000.00 Life insurance policy he has on her. He plots her death.

Jeff takes a contract out on his wife, for $15,000. Jeff states to the hired killer, "I do not want to know when or how you will kill my wife. Just do it!" Jeff gives the hit man half the money now and will give him the other half of the money after the job is completed.

Chapter 9

Jeff opens a new checking and savings account without Julie's name on them; He leaves her very little in the old accounts. Jeff also opens up accounts in Switzerland. This way she will never be able to get her hands on his money. Jeff is beginning to think of what else he could do to get her out of his life.

When Julie finds out about the money, she finds it hard to forgive Jeff. She will have to sell the mansion which she no longer can afford. Rachel would have to change schools again and deal with a change in neighborhoods. I will wait until the school year ends, then put this place up for sale. Julie never really got to know the neighbors. This place was a little too rich for her blood.

Julie focuses on her "Sewing Seeds" shop. She is so happy that she decided to open the shop up when there was still money left.

Many people come to console Julie because they know what Jeff was doing. Julie has become the topic of conversation in the small town. Julie keeps looking to God for strength.

Julie notices how the money has not only changed her husband but also changed the children.

Jerome is now addicted to gambling. All he thinks of is gambling. He is on a winning streak. As fast as he wins he spends the money on the people around him. He rents a beautiful penthouse overlooking the city. He loves the feeling of control. With the winning money he has acquired he lives like a king.

Julie used to see Jerome almost every day. He would check in on her and Rachel. He seldom stops by now and if he does stop in he is always in a hurry.

One day Jerome is absorb in the black jack tables in the casino. He loves being treated like royalty. Suddenly he starts to lose. Jerome is getting deeper and deeper in debt. Fear grips him and he believes his losing streak is only temporary. Jerome owes the house a lot of money. The mob is after him now. They worn Jerome that if the money is not paid back in a week they will kill him.

Jerome is hiding out in a cheap hotel on the other side of town. He calls his Dad and asks him to meet him to talk. Jeff meets him at a small cafe. Jerome asks him for more money and his Dad gives it to him. Jeff decided not to question why, because Jerome told him he would pay him back in a few days. Jeff can see the stress his son is under but doesn't bother to ask.

Jerome takes the money to a different casino across town knowing that he can win the money back. He plays the tables and loses it all in less than an hour. A few days later, Jerome has no choice but to call his Dad again and ask for more money. They meet, but Jeff refuses to give him more money. Jeff does not realize the serious trouble his son is in.

"I just gave you $20,000 and now you want another $20,000? get serious!!" His Dad says. "What do you need this money for?"

Jerome would not answer him. Jerome did not want his father to know about his addiction and the trouble that stemmed from it. Jerome knows he could win the money back if only he had some time.

Jerome pleads with his father and as they start to leave the cafe. Jeff looks up and notices the awesome full moon. So beautiful in all its spender. It reminded him of the moon he saw so many nights ago when they still lived in the little house. In the stillness of the night, shots ring out! The mob found Jerome. The bullets hit Jerome three times in the chest. Jeff grabs his son and holds him up against himself. Blood is everywhere, Jeff starts to rock his son in his arms and cries out "No, not my son!! "Not, my son!"

Jeff is in total despair he screams out, "First my sister, now my son!" He cannot control his tears. He reaches for the phone and dials 911 and then calls Julie and Jake. "Please come quickly!! Jerome is dying! He was shot three times by the mob!"

They meet at the hospital and Julie is overwhelmed with grief. She looks down on her first born baby, Jerome is dead! Words cannot describe the emptiness in her heart. Jerome is laying on the gurney so still. She cries out to Jeff and states, "Jerome and your sister would still be alive if it was not for your lust and greed for money."

"You fool!" screams Julie. "With all your money try to buy back Jerome's life. You can't!!!" Julie shouts. She falls on top of Jerome and cries out, "my baby, my baby."

Jake comes to the hospital. His eyes are dull from taking drugs all day. He looks at his parents and tries to focus on what is happening. He begins to cry. He goes up to his Mom and Dad and holds them close to him. Jake loved his brother, dearly. Jake had not seen his brother in months. He had no idea that his gambling had become a problem. Maybe if he would have returned Jerome's phone calls he would have confided in him about the addiction. Maybe if he did not cancel their lunch date last week they could have talked and he could have helped him. "Maybe....", Jake cried, "just maybe there was something I could have done!"

Chapter 10

The funeral was held a few days later and all the family was gathered in the cemetery. Jeff had gotten into politics and became important. His influence drew a lot of important people including the mayor, the Building Commissioner and the Building Administrator. Some of the people who attended the funeral were from the old neighborhood and saw Jerome grow up. Julie was so happy to see them again. Rachel and Jake stayed close to their Mom to offer her support. Jeff was withdrawn and stood by himself. He was feeling angry and blamed the doctors for not saving his son's life. Surely the ER people could have done something. The service began.

"We are gathered here today," says the pastor. "I have known Jeff and Julie and the children for years. Julie used to work for the church which I am sure everyone remembers."

Pastor continued His sermon. "We are here to celebrate life not death. I knew Jerome since he was a child. His love for the Lord shines throughout this community. When Jerome was little each year he would want to help us feed the homeless and give gifts to the children less fortunate than himself."

"I would be next to him while he wrapped and decorated the gifts he had for the children. He would volunteer his time every holiday. Jerome was part of the choir and would go and sing to nursing homes. He also visited the elderly church members."

"He was a young man who understood the meaning of giving. He was our example of giving of talents and time always helping one another. I have brought a picture of Jerome helping Mr. James, who is blind, cross the street. Jerome did not know I was watching him and taking a picture of his kind act."

"Anyone who knew Jerome, knew he was a man of God because he was not ashamed to tell people about Jesus Christ. One time a homeless man came to the church when Jerome was waiting for his mother to get off of work. I overheard him telling this man how much Jesus loved him and handed the man his own Bible. I was overjoyed to know that a youth in our church loved Jesus that much to offer his Bible to a man he did not know."

"These are just a few examples of things I noticed about Jerome, can you imagine how many things he did with no one watching?"

"I am sure Jerome is in heaven celebrating his new life with the God he so much loved."

Jeff is listening to the Pastor with his heart. How could he arrange the death of his wife and the mother of his children?

As the pastor continued to talk about Jerome, lurking behind the bushes is the hired killer Jeff paid pointing a gun at Julie.

"One shot to the head will kill this woman and I will be able to collect the rest of my money." stated the killer. Slowly he pulls the trigger. The bullet escapes the chamber and flies through the air and hits Julie in the head. "Jackpot!!!" the hired killer shouts and runs to his waiting car and drives away.

The crowd grasp in horror! Everyone looks around trying to figure out where the bullet came from.

Jake and Rachel were close to their Mom when the shots rang out. Jake caught his Mother as she fell over. The blood spills over the grave of Jerome.

Jeff runs and holds his wife and his two children close to him and starts to cry. All anger leaves Jeff. How could he get caught without God and family in his life?

People are in sheer panic, wondering if another bullet will come. They call 911 to report the gruesome killing of an innocent woman.

"How could this be?" everyone was whispering. This is the day their first born child is to be buried, now with the death of Julie, another grave, another senseless killing. No one could have even guessed a horrible thing like this to happen especially in a small town like this.

The police are asking questions and no one saw anything. No witness. The bullet came out of the bushes but no one seen anything. Not a person, not a car, everyone was focused on the service of Jerome. A man everyone loved. He was so kind and so generous. He truly will be missed. Now his mom is dead. The whole town was grieving on the death of not one but two townsfolk. The town has never seen anything like this before. Tears fill everyone's eyes.

After everything is over they return to their mansion on the hill. Rachel runs to her Daddy and brother. Hugging them, not wanting to let go. "I want my Mama! I want my Mama!"

Rachel looks at her Daddy and asks him to pray with her. She says with tears in her eyes "Mama always prays with me when I am afraid, Daddy I am so afraid without my Mama."

"Leave me alone!!!" Jeff states, "I cannot deal with another thing!"

Rachel cannot believe what she is hearing. This is not the Daddy she once loved. Jake pulls Rachel to his side and tells her everything will be alright. "I will take care of you," Jake confesses to his little sister. They head upstairs towards Rachel's room so she can lie down and rest. Angel jumps up on the bed next to her and licks her face. Rachel hugs Angel and tries to fall asleep. "Please stay with me," Rachel says to her brother Jake, "until I fall asleep."

Jake says, "I will stay with you." Rachel questions Jake, "Why would someone want to hurt Mama?" Jake did not know how to answer that. Jake whispers in Rachel ear, "Let the police figure it out, I am sure they will catch the person and we find out all the answers"

Rachel falls asleep and Jake goes downstairs. Jake thinks to himself, "I am the only one left that can stay with Rachel." Jake decides he will have to turn his life around and pick up where Mom left off. He will sell the mansion and take over the store so something good will come of this mess.

Jake is so mad at his Dad for not taking the responsibility of caring for his daughter. His Dad has become so mean and ugly that maybe it is better that he does not raise Rachel. Jake does not want Rachel around those people that his Dad hangs around with.

Jake cries out to the Lord, "Help!!!!!!"

Chapter 11

Jeff was alone thinking about what happened. Jeff is overwhelmed with guilt. His greed for wealth was all a deception. He truly thought that he would stay the same and be happy. His pride and greed caused the death of three people He loved dearly. His heart was torn apart. His money had gained nothing. Jeff looks up and sees the moon is full again. It is magnificent in all of its glory. It seems like the moon is the only consistent thing in his life.

A Scripture verse comes to Jeff's mind, Proverbs 13:7, "There is one who makes himself rich, yet has nothing...". I truly have nothing. I have lost God's favor. My family has lost respect for me.

Jeff sees himself and his wickedness for the first time since he had won the lottery. He saw what a crooked politician he had become when it was he who bribed the Zoning Administrator to change the zoning from residential to commercial. This way he and many others could make a large amount of money. He caused the death of two innocent people, Julie's parents. The deal sounded so good. He would make more money than he could dream of but Julie's parents would not do anything under the table to make it happen. Jeff got extremely angry at them and threatened their lives if they did not play ball. They were going to turn him over to the authorities. Jeff could not let this happen, so he stole a car and T boned them as they drove past the river. After Jeff hit them he pushed the car into the river where they both died.

Will God ever forgive Me?

Jeff no longer wants to live. He took the gun out of the desk drawer and pointed it to his head. He could not live with what he had caused. How could he have been so stupid? He failed his family and his God. Slowly he puts his finger on the trigger and gently squeezes the trigger. He looks forward to the end. The end of everything, his life, his guilt and his time on this planet. In slow motion he sees himself dying.

Suddenly the alarm went off! Jeff opened his eyes! His wife laying next to him asleep. It was only a dream! Jeff jumped out of bed and began to dance!

The announcer on the radio says, "Buy your lottery ticket today, grand prize $500 million dollars."

Jeff turned off the radio and said, "God has given me a second chance! It is a wonderful morning!! Lord I give you praise and honor for being my God! I promise you I will be your faithful servant, now and forever! I will put my trust in you always!"

The End

or

Is it the beginning?

Manufactured by Amazon.ca
Acheson, AB

15238300R00049